THE HEART OF MIDLOTHIAN

WALTER SCOTT

www.realreads.co.uk

Retold by Margaret Elphinstone
Illustrated by Ken Laidlaw

Published by Real Reads Ltd
Stroud, Gloucestershire, UK
www.realreads.co.uk

Text copyright © Margaret Elphinstone 2012
Illustrations copyright © Ken Laidlaw 2012
The right of Margaret Elphinstone to be identified as author of
this book has been asserted by her in accordance with the
Copyright, Design and Patents Act 1988

First published in 2012

All rights reserved
No part of this publication may be reproduced or transmitted in any
form or by any means, electronic or mechanical, including
photocopy, recording, or any information storage and retrieval
system, without permission in writing from the publisher.

ISBN 978-1-906230-41-8

Printed in Singapore by Imago Ltd
Designed by Lucy Guenot
Typeset by Bookcraft Ltd, Stroud, Gloucestershire

CONTENTS

The Characters   4

The Heart of Midlothian   7

Taking things further   55

THE CHARACTERS

Jeanie Deans

Jeanie is a strictly-brought-up country girl. She could save her sister by telling a lie. But will she?

Effie Deans

Jeanie's beautiful but wilful sister gives birth to a child in secret. Will she be hanged for child murder?

David Deans

Jeanie and Effie's father once fought for religious freedom. But will his God help him now?

Reuben Butler

Reuben is a poor minister. Jeanie loves him, but believes she'd wrong him if she married him.

4

George Robertson

Smuggler, rioter, Effie's lover and a fugitive – who is the mysterious George Robertson, and what will happen to him?

Madge Wildfire and Meg Murdockson

What made Madge Wildfire insane? What is her mother, Meg, really up to? These two are keeping a vital secret.

Mr and Mrs Saddletree

The Saddletrees have a shop near the Grassmarket, a good place for the latest gossip.

The Duke of Argyll and Queen Caroline

The Duke of Argyll is a powerful Scottish courtier in London, but he's out of favour with Queen Caroline.

THE HEART OF MIDLOTHIAN

Jeanie Deans gazed across the fields towards the road from Edinburgh. In one field her father was feeding the cattle. He'd be angry if her sister wasn't back for evening prayers.

At last a figure appeared. Not one person, but two. One of them drew back hastily behind the field wall. The other climbed the stile. It was Effie.

'Effie! Where hae ye been sae late at e'en?'

'It's no late, lass,' answered Effie.

'It's chappit eight on every clock in town! And who was that parted wi you at the stile?'

'Naebody.'

'Naebody?'

'What needs ye aye speering at folk?' retorted Effie. 'And what about Reuben Butler the school dominie aye coming here? Will you tell me he comes to see our father? Or is it ye he comes to see, Jeanie?' Effie saw that Jeanie was upset. She flung her arms round her neck, and kissed her.

'I canna be muckle vexed wi anything ye say to me,' said Jeanie, hurt though she was. 'But oh – dinna vex our father!'

'I will not,' replied Effie. 'And if there were as many dances the morn's night as there are merry dancers in the sky on a frosty night, I winna gang near ane o' them.'

'Dance! Oh Effie, what could take ye to a dance?'

David Deans, coming from the byre, overheard this. 'Dance, said ye! Don't name such a word at my door! It's a wicked pastime. I bless God that in the days when I could have danced, I was fighting for the freedom to worship God in our own way in Scotland. I lived in dread of bloody rope and swift bullet. I fought an English government that wanted us in Scotland to have bishops, and masses, and all kinds of evil which we Presbyterians know to be wrong. Let me hear no more of dancing, or singing, or such wickedness, ever again.'

Both daughters were crying now. 'Let's go in to our prayers now, and we'll seek god's grace to preserve us from all manner of sins.'

Effie had meant to confide in Jeanie when she came home. But now she was angry. 'Jeanie would think me nae better than the dirt under her feet, if I told her I'd danced with him four times on the green,' she thought. 'And she'd tell father. But I'll no go there again. It would be wrong.'

After her stepmother died, Jeanie had brought up Effie as best she could. Although David Deans was a strict Presbyterian, he'd always been gentle with his beautiful younger daughter. The previous year a distant relative, Mrs Saddletree, had offered Effie a job in her husband's Edinburgh shop. Effie would lodge with the family and worship with them at the Tolbooth Kirk every Sabbath. Deans didn't know that Mrs Saddletree was now very ill in bed. No one was keeping an eye on young Effie amid the temptations of the capital city.

Jeanie was more worried about Effie than David was. When Effie left next morning, Jeanie begged her to take care. Effie sobbed and kissed her sister, promising to take her advice to heart, and so they parted.

Some months later Reuben Butler, the young man Effie had teased Jeanie about, arrived in Edinburgh. Although he was a minister of the church he had no parish, so he'd found work as a schoolmaster, a very badly paid profession. Butler needed a new bridle rein so he went to the Saddletrees' shop in the West Bow. This was close to the Grassmarket where public hangings regularly took place in front of large crowds, and not far from the Tolbooth prison, which Edinburgh folk called the Heart of Midlothian. Butler found the

Saddletrees and their neighbours gossiping about the most recent hanging. Mr Saddletree loved talking about the law and executions.

Butler overheard a neighbour woman say, 'Ye mind the gude auld time before the Union with England? Scotland was Scotland in those days. This Captain Porteous wouldn't have got away wi' it back then. But that's twenty year ago now.'

'Ah, Mr Butler!' Saddletree welcomed him. 'What do you think of this stramash about Porteous?'

'Porteous? Isn't he the captain of the city guard?'

'Ye've no heard? Well it all started with that smuggler – Wilson – who was ruined because the customs officers stopped him smuggling. Wilson thought they owed him something, so he and young Robertson – whoever he may be – robbed the Collector of Customs of a great sum of money seized from the smugglers. Wilson thought of the money as his own.'

'Which it was not!'

'Wait, Mr Butler, there's more. Ye ken how the condemned prisoners are taken to the Tolbooth

Kirk on the Sabbath before they're hanged? Well
they caught Wilson and Robertson, and they were
condemned. But at the kirk, this Wilson – a big,
strong man he was – seized the two guards, one
with each hand, and called to Robertson, "Run,
Geordie, run!" Young Robertson gathered his wits
just in time. He ran – and was lost in the crowd.
Captain Porteous was furious that his soldiers had
been outwitted, and when he heard there was a
plan to rescue Wilson from the gallows, he was
angrier still. He treated Wilson cruelly — he had
him hanged as fast as he could, before he'd even
said his prayers.

'As Wilson's body swung on the gibbet, folk
began throwing stones at the soldiers. Porteous

seized a musket and shot a man dead, then he ordered the soldiers to fire on the mob. The soldiers killed half a dozen and more were wounded. It was all Porteous could do to get his men back to the guard-house.'

'Here, on the streets of Edinburgh! That's outrageous!'

'Porteous tried to lie his way out of it – said he'd never ordered the soldiers to fire. Not true – dozens heard him. So the Lords passed sentence of death against him, to be hanged in the Grassmarket on the 8th of September of this year 1736, for wilful murder!'

'Which is what he deserves,' put in Mrs Saddletree. 'But then … '

'I'll tell him!' interrupted Saddletree. 'Everyone came to see Porteous' execution. Every place in the Grassmarket – all the windows, every foot of ground – was filled with spectators. The gibbet with the halter dangling from it was ready and waiting.'

'If an Edinburgh mob's roused, they're the fiercest in Europe,' put in Butler.

'Ah Mr Butler, but they werena fierce. They were waiting, stern and silent, to see justice done. And when it wasna ... '

'Porteous wasn't hanged?'

'No! The magistrates had petitioned the King to pardon Porteous. Those in power always stick together! The King's messenger came from Queen Caroline in London – the King was away – just as they were taking Porteous to be hanged. A reprieve! And the crowds had gathered, and the gibbet was set up ready in the Grassmarket, where it's standing yet. There could have been a riot, like in the old days we all remember! It's a mercy the crowd dispersed so peacefully. But I don't think we've heard the last of it yet,' concluded Mr Saddletree.

'I canna be thinking of that gibbet, but I think of puir Effie Deans,' broke in his wife, 'She's lying in that same Heart of Midlothian prison as that wicked Porteous. A servant lass of ours, Mr Butler, and as innocent a lass ... puir Effie used to help me tumble the bundles of leather up and down, and range out the goods.'

Butler looked horrified. 'You don't mean Effie – David Deans' daughter?'

'Ay, Jeanie Deans' sister. Jeanie was here just now about the matter. Effie was to be tried for murder by now, but they put it off because of the Porteous case. But what's the matter wi' you, Mr Butler. Ye're as white as a sheet. Will ye take a dram?'

'By no means. I walked from Dumfries yesterday, and it's a warm day, that's all. But Effie! To be tried for murder! How? Why?'

15

'Puir Effie!' said Mrs Saddletree. 'The lass had a child, but told no one. I was laid up ill so long, I didna ken! She had the bairn in secret. Maybe it was still-born. Maybe it's alive at this moment. Effie says she disna ken. But if she can't produce the bairn, the law says she murdered it, though there's no proof of it. A wicked law!'

'The King made the statute,' said Saddletree, 'to prevent the horrid crime of bringing forth children in secret.'

'But not murder! They can't prove she murdered the bairn, and yet they'll hang her!'

'I must go! I must see a lawyer at once!' Butler rushed out of the shop.

'What has he to do wi Effie?' asked Saddletree, staring after him.

'You remember – his mother is tenant of the land alongside Davie Deans'. Young Butler grew up with Jeanie Deans. I'll wager he'd marry Jeanie the morn if he had any money. Maybe he can help Effie, but I doubt it.'

By nightfall, Butler had still failed to find a lawyer. Perhaps he could speak to Effie herself. He stopped before the Heart of Midlothian in the centre of the High Street. He knocked at the stout gate and asked the turnkey if he could see Effie Deans.

'I can't let you in, sir. We're locking up early.'

'On account of your other prisoner – Captain Porteous?'

The turnkey looked hard at Butler, but said nothing, then fastened the gate with a plate of strong steel over the keyhole.

Butler went down through the Grassmarket, deep in thought. He didn't notice the jostling crowds surrounding him until a man wearing a woman's shawl and bonnet stopped him.

'Are you a clergyman?'

'I ... yes ... but I'm not a placed minister. I have no parish.'

'Come with us!'

'Why?'

'You'll find out.'

The people forced Butler to go with them

round the city gates – the West Port, the Cowgate and the Netherport. The man who'd spoken to him seemed to be in charge. They called him Madge Wildfire – surely not his real name? The crowd seized the guards and closed the city gates so no one could leave the city. They stormed into the guardhouse, grabbing the weapons inside: guns, bayonets, long Lochaber axes.

'Porteous! Porteous!' they cried. 'To the Tolbooth!'

Butler was carried along with them. The rioters told terrified ladies in their carriages to hurry home. They chased away messengers sent by the magistrates, but never harmed them. Such restraint was unlike the usual violent Edinburgh mob. These men were clearly obeying orders. But whose? They reached the prison.

Butler watched in horror as the mob attacked the door. In no time they'd made a huge bonfire. Flames roared and crackled. The door gave way. As the flames died down man after man bounded over the glowing embers.

Porteous was dragged from the Tolbooth, so violently that Butler feared they'd kill him on the spot.

'Hang the murderer! To the Grassmarket with him!'

'Where's that clergyman?' called the leader. 'You – minister – walk beside him. Prepare him for immediate death! As for you, Porteous – make your peace with heaven!'

'You can't do this!' cried Butler. 'He may deserve death, but you are neither judge nor jury. The laws of God ... '

'Cut your sermon short, or we'll hang you up beside him! Blood must have blood!'

Butler was forced to walk by Porteous as they carried him down to the gallows. 'Are you prepared for this dreadful end?' he asked in a faltering voice. 'Oh, turn to God ... '

'I'm a soldier,' said Porteous sullenly. 'They'll murder me. My sins as well as my blood can lie at their door.'

Butler was separated from Porteous just before the gallows. As he fled he heard a shout of triumph. He cast back a terrified glance, and, by the dusky red light of the torches, saw a figure struggling as it hung suspended above the heads of the multitude. Filled with horror, he turned and ran.

Towering over Edinburgh's Holyrood Palace are the Salisbury Crags, a wild and lonely place for a man to hide. Butler came cautiously down from the crags at dawn, into a deep, grassy valley scattered with huge rocks. As he hurried towards David Deans' farm, he was stopped by a young man.

'Do you know the farm yonder?' the stranger asked him. 'A woman lives there – Jeanie Deans. You're walking that way. Will you give her a message?'

'What!' cried Butler. 'Jeanie Deans!'

'You know her? Tell her I'll be at Muschat's Cairn tonight, as the moon rises. Tell her she must come!'

'Who are you?'

'I'm the devil! But give my message!'

In Deans' cottage, Butler found the old man seated by the fire with his well-worn pocket Bible in his hands. He was bowed down by Effie's fall, and he couldn't look Butler in the face.

Butler clasped his hand. 'God comfort you – God comfort you!'

Jeanie wept for her sister, but mingled with those tears were bitter drops of grief for her own degradation. When she and Butler were alone she told him, 'Reuben, I have to tell ye – we canna be married now. It's best for baith our sakes.'

'Why?' cried Butler. 'Effie's disgrace lies neither at your door nor mine. It's an evil of God's sending. It can't break the promises we made to each other.'

'Reuben, I ken weel that ye think mair of me than yourself. Ye are bred to God's ministry. Men say ye will some day rise high in the Kirk. This stain won't ever be forgotten, as lang as our heads are abune the ground.' Jeanie burst into tears.

Nothing Butler could say would move her. Did she no longer love him? Butler remembered the man he'd met. 'I'm charged with a message to you, Jeanie.'

'What can ony ane have to say to me?'

'It's from a stranger. A young man I met this morning. He said you must meet him alone at Muschat's Cairn this night, as soon as the moon rises.' Butler looked at her fixedly, much displeased.

'Then I shall certainly go!'

Poor Jeanie had brought herself to bear parting with Reuben for ever, but she'd never thought they'd part in unkindness. When the moon rose she

crept from the house. Dim cliffs and scattered rocks loomed in the moonlight below Salisbury Crags. Jeanie's mind was filled with stories of witches and demons. A man rose suddenly from behind Muschat's Cairn. Jeanie almost screamed aloud.

'Are you the sister of Effie Deans?' he demanded.

'Yes I am. Tell me how we can save her!'

'You can save her, if you listen. She trusted me, but I've destroyed her, and the innocent child that was born to me!'

'Then you are the wicked cause of my sister's ruin?'

'I'm the father of her child.'

'I pray God to forgive you.'

'If you like,' he replied. 'Only promise to do what I say, and save your sister's life.'

'How?'

'I can't come forward. I'm fleeing from the law, twice over. A friend helped me to escape being hanged. And last night I was ... Never mind. Will you save your sister?'

'Tell me she's innocent – she didn't murder her child?'

'Of course she didn't! I can guess who took the child. But listen: naturally your sister would tell you she was expecting a baby. You only have to swear to it in court. The law assumes she murdered her baby because she kept it secret. If she told someone, then it proves she wasn't concealing the birth. It proves she wasn't planning to murder the baby. So she won't be hanged.'

'But Effie never did tell me.'

'Don't be dull! That's not the point. You only have to say that she did before these Justices.'

'But I can't! Effie's blamed for concealing her condition: she did conceal it. I'd be lying if I said she'd told me.'

'So you don't want to save your sister from being murdered? You don't care if she's hanged for a crime she didn't commit?'

Jeanie wept in bitter agony. 'Of course I want to save her! But I canna change right into wrang, or make that true which is false.'

'Who's that?' he said suddenly. 'Someone's coming!

I can't stay. Your sister's fate is in your hands!' With
that he vanished into the darkness.

Butler stood before the blackened doorless gateway
of the Tolbooth. He was so preoccupied with his
meeting with the mysterious stranger and his
agitating conversation with Jeanie that for the
moment he'd forgotten all about yesterday's riot. He
didn't even see that the prison was strongly defended
with extra soldiers. He asked if he could see Effie
Deans.

'I think,' said the turnkey, 'ye'll be the same lad
that was in for to see her yestreen?'

'Yes.'

'And ye speered at me if we locked up earlier on
account of Porteous?'

'Very likely. Can I see Effie Deans?'

'Gang in by, up the turnpike stair, and turn left.'

Butler entered the room as he'd been told.
The door slammed behind him, and the key turned
in the lock. 'What's this?' he called. 'I came to see

Effie Deans. Let me out! I'm a minister – Reuben Butler.'

'I ken that weel eneugh. The sheriff officers are out seeking ye, for your part in the riot yestreen.'

Soon afterwards, Jeanie arrived at the Tolbooth to see Effie. She had no idea that now Butler was a prisoner there too.

When Jeanie entered Effie's cell, Effie threw herself on her sister's neck. 'Jeanie! Jeanie! It's lang since I hae seen ye!'

Both sisters wept bitterly.

'Oh Effie! How could you hide your condition from me? Had ye but spoke ae word – '

'And what gude would that hae dune?'

'Oh,' sobbed Jeanie, 'If I were free to swear that ye had said but ae word of how it stood wi ye, they couldna have touched your life this day.'

'Could they na?' Effie's interest was awakened. 'Wha tauld ye that? Was it him? Was it George? George Robertson? Oh, I see it was him. Poor lad.'

'And ye have suffered a' this for him, and ye can think of loving him still?' said her sister, in a voice betwixt pity and blame.

'But Jeanie – the poor innocent new-born wee ane! Oh can ye find out wha has taken it away, and what they hae done wi't? What did George say to ye?'

Jeanie sighed, and told Effie what Robertson had said to her at Muschat's Cairn.

'If ye say this to yon folks, it wad save my life? And ye told him ye would do it?'

'I tauld him,' replied Jeanie, trembling, 'That I daured na swear to a lie.'

'But ye ken I'd never murder my ain bairn!'

'Of course ye didna! But to say that ye tauld me anything would be a lie. It would be a sin.'

The turnkey rattled his keys at the door.

Effie sobbed. 'I'm thinking now about a high, black gibbet, and a sea of faces all looking up at puir Effie Deans! I see puir George Robertson, and that Meg Murdockson laughing at me, and telling me I'd seen the last of my wean – it's all confused, Jeanie. God preserve me, that old woman has a fearsome face!'

'What old woman? Oh Effie, look up, and say what ye wad hae me do. I could find it in my heart almost to say that I wad do't.'

'No, Jeanie. I'm better minded now. We have to part. Ye'll come back and see me before – ' Here she stopped, and became deadly pale.

As she left, Jeanie heard the jarring bolts turn upon her sister.

Reuben heard them too, but he had no idea that it was Jeanie who passed his cell. When the turnkey opened his door, he leapt up eagerly. The magistrate had come to the jail, and Butler was to appear before him immediately. He found the magistrate sitting at a table in a private room. The officer also brought in a young woman of about eighteen, dressed fantastically in a blue riding-jacket with tarnished lace, a Highland bonnet, and a bunch of broken feathers. She was handsome in a coarse way, with bright, wild-looking black eyes.

She dropped a curtsey to the magistrate. 'Here's poor Madge brought off the street by a grand officer. This is honour on earth, for ance!' And off she went into a song: 'Hey for cavaliers, ho for cavaliers ... '

'Did you ever see this madwoman before?' said the magistrate to Butler.

'Not to my knowledge, sir,' replied Butler.

'That is Madge Wildfire, as she calls herself.'

31

'Ay, that I am,' said Madge, 'And that I have been ever since I was ... something better.' She began to sing again:

I glance like the wildfire through country and town;
I'm seen on the causeway – I'm seen on the down;
The lightning that flashes for bright and so free,
Is scarcely so blithe or so bonny as me.

'Haud yer tongue, ye skirling limmer!' said the officer.

'Let her alone,' said the magistrate. 'But first Mr Butler, take another look of her. What think ye now?'

'As I did before,' said Butler, 'that I never saw the poor demented creature in my life before.'

'Then she is not the person that the rioters were calling Madge Wildfire?'

'Certainly not. That was a man in woman's clothes.'

'That was Geordie Robertson put on my ilka-day's clothes on his ain bonny self yestreen, and gaed through the town wi' them, and grand he lookit, like ony queen in the land.' And Madge sang,

What did ye wi' the bridal ring –
bridal ring – bridal ring ... ?

'Hear that, officer? And this same Robertson tried to get Effie Deans to break jail last night. Ae thing I'm sure of – Robertson was the father of Effie Deans' bairn. If we can get her to admit it ... '

'Would it save her?' broke in Butler eagerly.

The magistrate ignored him, and spoke to the officer. 'It's a cruel law. A child may have been born. It may have been taken away while the mother was unconscious. It may have died of hunger without its mother. But if Effie Deans is found guilty at her trial, execution will follow. But we're no here to speak o' that. I'll go and talk to Effie's father when the hurry of this Porteous investigation is over.'

'Is Mr Butler to remain in prison meanwhile?'

'For the present, certainly.' The magistrate turned to Butler. 'I've made enquiries about you. Your private character is excellent, and you only arrived in Edinburgh yesterday. You couldn't have had any part in planning the riot. But the fact remains ... what's that knocking?'

The turnkey went out, and returned a moment later. 'It's Madge's mother – old Meg Murdockson.'

A haggard old woman pushed past him into the room. 'I want my bairn!' she screamed. 'Gie me back my puir crazy bairn!'

'She wants her daughter, sir,' said the turnkey. 'Madge Wildfire.'

The magistrate looked at Meg Murdockson with disfavour. 'I suppose her child may be as dear to her as to a more amiable mother. We've clarified that Madge Wildfire was not involved in the riots. Let her return home with her mother.'

Meg Murdockson pushed her daughter violently towards the door. Meg waved her hand wildly and sang at the top of her voice as she was led away,

Up in the air, on my bonny grey mare,
And I see ... and I see ... and I see —

The mob jostled round the court-house door. Effie's trial had become notorious and everyone had come to see. The crowd laughed and joked and quarrelled as if they were assembled for a holiday. Deans and Jeanie could hardly push their way through.

'Look at the ruling elder!' someone jeered at them. 'He's come to see a precious sister glorify God, by hanging in the Grassmarket!'

'Whist, shame in ye, sirs,' someone reproved him. 'It's her father and sister.'

All fell back to make way for David Deans and his daughter. Even the rudest were struck with shame and silence.

Deans chose a seat right at the back of the court.

Jeanie had to leave him to go into the separate room where witnesses waited until they were called into the court. The five Lords of Justiciary, in their long scarlet robes, took their places upon the bench.

The audience rose to receive them. Shouts from the mob outside heralded the arrival of the prisoner. Effie was brought in and placed between two guards with fixed bayonets, as a prisoner at the bar.

'Euphemia Deans,' said the presiding Judge. 'Stand up, and listen to the criminal indictment against you.'

Effie cast a bewildered look at the crowd.

'Put back your hair, Effie,' said one of the officers, for Effie, as an unmarried woman, wore no cap, and she no longer dared to wear the ribband which implied that she was a maiden. Her long hair hung in tangles over her face. She pushed it back with a trembling hand.

She barely heard the counsel for the crown talking about the crime of infanticide, and the law that had been made to deal with it. When the counsel for the crown stopped talking at last, the counsel for the prisoner – the man who was there to defend her – got up and made his speech. He ended by saying, ' ... I can prove that the prisoner spoke to her sister about her condition. She never tried to conceal her condition. She was very ill when she gave birth. While she had a fever, the wretched woman who acted as midwife deceived her, and carried off the baby. It may have been murdered for all I know.'

Effie uttered a piercing shriek.

'My lords,' said the counsel, 'the prisoner's distress at my words proves that she was not the murderer.'

The counsel for the prisoner then called Jeanie Deans as witness.

Jeanie came in, slowly following the court officer. Effie started up, hands outstretched. 'Oh Jeanie!' she cried. 'Save me, save me!'

Jeanie wept bitterly. The judge told her to compose herself, and swear the oath: 'the truth to tell, and no truth to conceal, as far as she knew or should be asked.' Jeanie repeated the oath in a low but distinct voice.

'Young woman,' said the judge. 'It is impossible not to pity the circumstances in which you come before this court. Yet it is my duty to tell you that the truth is what you owe to your country and to God, whose word is truth.'

The counsel for the prisoner asked her, 'You are the sister of the prisoner?'

'Yes, sir.'

He questioned her about Effie going to Edinburgh and working for the Saddletrees.

'And you noticed that she didn't seem as well as usual?'

'Yes, sir.'

'Did you ask her why she was unwell?'

'I asked her what ailed her.'

'And what answer did she give?'

Jeanie was silent, and looked deadly pale.

'Take courage, young woman. I asked what your sister said ailed her, when you asked.'

'Nothing,' said Jeanie faintly.

'Nothing? You mean nothing at first?'

'Alack, alack!' cried Jeanie. 'She never breathed word to me about it.'

A deep groan passed through the court. David Deans cried out.

'Let me gang to my father,' cried Jeanie. 'I will gang to him.'

Effie watched her father and sister leave the court. Then she addressed the court with more courage than she had shown yet. 'My Lords, if it's your pleasure to gang on wi' this matter, the weariest day will hae its end at last.'

The trial wound slowly to its end. The jury came back with their verdict. The punishment was read out: Effie Deans was to return to the Tolbooth prison in Edinburgh until the day, when betwixt two and four o'clock in the afternoon, she was to be conveyed to the place of execution, and there hanged by the neck upon a gibbet.

'And this,' finished the Doomster who read out the judgement, 'I pronounce for Doom.'

'Is there no hope?' Jeanie asked Mrs Saddletree, her cheeks as pale as ashes. They were sitting beside the Saddletrees' spare bed, where David Deans lay senseless, overcome by his daughter's sentence.

'Next to nane,' said Mrs Saddletree. Unless she gets the King's mercy, as Porteous did.'

'Porteous? Of course!' Jeanie leapt to her feet.

'Mrs Saddletree, will ye look to my father? I must go!'

'Will ye no stay wi' him, Jeanie, bairn?'

'I canna. I will go to London, and beg her pardon from the King and Queen. If they pardoned Porteous, they may pardon her. If a sister asks a sister's life on her bended knees, they will pardon her. They shall pardon her. God bless you! Take care of my father!'

'Ah Jeanie, wait! London is a thousand miles from this, far ayont the saut sea.'

'It is no sae far. They go to it by land. Reuben Butler told me sae.'

When Jeanie spoke to Mr Saddletree, he had a better idea. 'There's some chance of your carrying the day. But you must not go to the King until you have some friend at court. Try the Duke of Argyll – he's Scotland's friend. I ken the great folks dinna muckle like him – but they fear him and that will serve your purpose just as weel. And ye'll need to stay in London – I'll give you the direction of Mrs Glass, a cousin of ours in the city.

She'll help you if she can. Now,' – he put a purse
into her hand – 'There's guineas for ye.'

'God bless you, Mr Saddletree!'

With a strong heart, Jeanie Deans, walking at
the rate of twenty miles a-day, crossed southern
Scotland, entered England and got as far as
Durham. Up until now she'd been among her
own countryfolk, or northerners among whom her
bare feet and tartan plaid attracted no attention.
As she went further people began to sneer at her
clothes. She put her plaid in her bundle, and began
to wear shoes and stockings all day. It seemed
very extravagant, and the shoes hurt her feet.
Whenever she spoke folk mocked her accent and

her language, so she said as little as possible. But she never lacked food or shelter for the night. Sometimes she got a ride in a waggon for part of the way. Sometimes the landlords refused payment, saying, 'Thee hast a long way afore thee, lass, and I'd never take penny out o' a single woman's purse.'

One day, about a fortnight after Jeanie left Edinburgh, the Duke of Argyll was alone in his splendid library in London, when a servant informed him that a country girl from Scotland wished to speak to him.

'A country girl, and from Scotland!' repeated

the Duke. 'What can have brought her to London? Well, show her up.'

The Duke saw a rather short, sunburnt, freckled young woman enter the room.

'Did you wish to speak to me, my bonny lass? I guess by your dress, you are just come from poor old Scotland. Did you walk through the London streets in your tartan plaid?'

'No sir, Mrs Glass brought me in her carriage. Sir, I am the sister of that poor unfortunate criminal, Effie Deans, who is ordered for execution.'

'Ah, I've heard that unhappy story.'

'I've come up frae the north to see what could be done for her in the way of getting a pardon.'

'Alas, my poor girl. You have made a long and sad journey to very little purpose.'

'But there's a law for reprieving her, if it is in the King's pleasure.'

'Certainly there is. But the King and Queen are very angry about the disorders in Edinburgh. They pardoned Porteous, and the Edinburgh mob took the law into their own hands and hanged him. I'm out of favour myself as a result. I can't avert your sister's fate. She must die.'

'We must a' die, sir. But we shouldna hasten ilk other out o' the world. Your honour kens that better than me.'

'It is the law of God and man that the murderer must surely die.'

'But sir, Effie canna be proved to be a murderer. And if she be not, and the law takes her life anyway, wha is it that is the murderer then?'

'I own I think your sister's case is a very hard one.'

'God bless you sir, for that word!'

'It's against the spirit of British law to take for granted what is not proved, or to punish with death a crime which may not have been committed at all. Leave this with me. You shall hear from me. Be ready to come at a moment's warning. And please to be dressed just as you are at present. Now do not hope too much from what I have promised. I will do my best, but God has the hearts of kings in his own hand.'

The Duke's coach came for Jeanie two days later. It drove her out into the country, until they reached a great park below a castle on a hill. The Duke himself was there to meet her.

'This is braw rich feeding for the cows,' said Jeanie, looking around.

The Duke smiled. 'Come with me.'

They crossed the stately grounds and entered a narrow walk with hedges on each side. Two ladies were walking towards them. 'Don't be afraid,'

said the Duke. 'When I've spoken to them, step forward and make your plea.'

Jeanie couldn't catch all that followed, but she heard the Duke say, 'I think mercy in this case would win back the loyalty of his Majesty's good subjects in Scotland.'

The Queen didn't like that. 'That his Majesty has good subjects in England, my lord Duke, he thanks God and the law. That he has subjects in Scotland – I think he may thank God and his sword!'

The Duke flushed, but he went on talking quietly.

Jeanie heard the Queen say. 'How dare you ask this? I have had enough of Scotch pardons!'

That was all she heard until the Duke beckoned her forward.

'You have walked all the way from Scotland?' the Queen asked Jeanie. 'How far can you walk in a day?'

'Five and twenty miles and a bittock.'

'And a what?'

'About five miles more,' put in the Duke.

'And I thought I was a good walker! You must have had a very tiring journey. And to little purpose, I fear, since, if the King were to pardon your sister, no doubt your people of Edinburgh would hang her themselves, out of spite!'

'I'm sure that baith town and country wad rejoice to see his Majesty taking compassion on a poor unfriended creature.'

'His Majesty did not find it so with Porteous,' said the Queen.

'If it like you, madam,' said Jeanie, 'I would hae gaen to the end of the earth to save Porteous, or any other unhappy man. But he is dead and gane to his place. But my puir sister Effie still lives! She still lives, and a word of the king's mouth might restore her to her broken-hearted auld father. My father never forgot to pray for his Majesty.

'O, madam, if ever ye kenned what it was to sorrow for a sinning and a suffering creature, have some compassion on our misery! Save an honest house from dishonour, and an unhappy girl, not eighteen years of age, from an early and dreadful death! Alas, it is not when we sleep soft and wake merry that we think on other people's sufferings. But when the hour of trouble comes – and seldom may it visit your Leddyship – and when the hour of death comes – and it comes to high and low – lang and late may it be yours – oh my Leddy, then it isna what we hae dune for oursells, but what we hae dune for others, that we think on maist pleasantly. And the thought that ye spared the puir thing's life will be sweeter in that hour, come when it may, than if ye could hang the haill Porteous mob at the tail of a tow.'

The tears poured down Jeanie's cheeks as she made her plea.

'This is eloquence,' said the Queen to Argyll. 'Young woman, I cannot grant a pardon to your sister, but I can warmly petition his Majesty to do so. You have saved your sister's life.'

The Queen took an embroidered needlecase from her lady-in-waiting. 'This is for you, young woman, as a memento of this occasion. Open it when you get home.'

Reuben Butler was a free man again, cleared of all
suspicion. The meeting between him and Jeanie was
more remarkable for its simple sincerity than for great
expression of feeling. The Queen's needle-case had
contained a note for £50, and the Duke of Argyll was
to give Butler a parish in his own country of Argyll.
David Deans gave his blessing to their marriage. Their
happiness would have been complete were it not for
Effie.

Effie had been freed as soon as the pardon arrived
from London. She went back to her father's house
and stayed there two nights. On the third night she
disappeared. No one knew what had become of her until
an ill-spelt letter arrived for Jeanie, written at sea, saying
she should bear the burden of her disgrace alone. She
could not bear the way her father cast up her sins to her.
She should never see Jeanie ony mair, but she would
pray for her night and day, baith for what she had done,
and for what she scorned to do, on Effie's behalf.

It was clear that Effie had run off with Robertson. Only that would explain why she had gone abroad. Robertson had to stay away from Scotland until his part in the affair of Porteous was totally forgotten.

The letter ended, 'Farewell, my dearest Jeanie. Do not show this even to Mr Butler, much less to anyone else. They would judge me too hardly. Your sister, Effie.'

Robertson married Effie. They lived a wandering life on the continent, and had no more children. Reuben Butler and Jeanie lived for the rest of their lives on the Duke's estates in Argyll, where David Deans joined them in his old age. Happy in each other, in the prosperity of their growing family, and the love and honour of all who knew them, this simple pair lived beloved, and died lamented.

The boy looked back at the tobacco plantations enclosed by miles of rail fencing. For four years – or was it five – he'd worked in those hot fields, slave to a cruel master. They called the boy an indentured servant, but really he was a slave. And now he'd killed his master. Each time he thought of the killing he laughed out loud. They'd hang him if they caught him. But he had friends among the Indians. They knew a better way to live. No white man would ever hear of him again.

He pushed his shaggy hair out of his eyes, and gazed west. He had no name. They used to call him the Whistler, but he'd left that name behind when the shipmaster sold him to the American traders. That was in ... Argyll. A long-ago name; he could barely remember. Before that there had been the wandering and begging, cold and hunger, and sometimes Madge singing.

Madge Wildfire. Not the old woman Murdockson – she didn't matter. He remembered the outline of the gallows against the sky. She'd looked like a spider twitching at the end of a thread. No more curses and beatings from her; he'd been glad to see her die. But Madge had died of grief. And yet old Murdockson treated her daughter worse than anyone. Why should Madge care? Or did Madge lose her mind because they ducked her in the muddy pool, to see whether she were a witch or no?

He'd stayed beside Madge in the hospital. There was a row of beds, all empty except for Madge's. She sang, just as she'd always done,

Cauld is my bed, Lord Archibald,
And sad my sleep of sorrow ...

A long time ago Madge used to tell him the story. The story was about his real mother, the one with the long hair, from whom he was stolen away. Either they hanged her when he was lost, or they forgot to hang her. Madge wasn't his mother. Meg stole him because he should never have been born. His father belonged to Madge, and to Madge's baby that died, and his father went away and took Madge's mind away with him too, so she couldn't remember, and old Mother Murdockson, who could remember, would never tell him anything anyway.

There was no need now to remember. Only bits of the songs stayed with him. The song Madge sang when she was dying. He couldn't forget that however hard he tried.

Even where he was going now, he knew the song would come too:

> *Proud Maisie is in the wood,*
> > *Walking so early:*
> *Sweet Robin sits on the bush,*
> > *Singing so rarely.*
>
> *'Tell me, thou bonny bird,*
> > *When shall I marry me?'*
> *'When six braw gentlemen*
> > *Kirkward shall carry ye.'*
>
> *'Who makes the bridal bed,*
> > *Birdie, say truly?'*
> *'The grey-headed sexton,*
> > *That delves the grave duly.'*
>
> *The glow-worm o'er grave and stone*
> > *Shall light thee steady;*
> *The owl from the steeple sing,*
> > *'Welcome, proud lady.'*

TAKING THINGS FURTHER
The real read

This *Real Reads* version of *The Heart of Midlothian* is a retelling of Walter Scott's original book. If you would like to read the full novel in all its glory, many complete editions are available, from bargain paperbacks to beautifully bound hardbacks. You could find a copy in your local charity shop, or in your library.

Filling in the spaces

Scott's *The Heart of Midlothian* encompasses a very broad sweep of history, depicting events and exploring issues that show the reader what Scotland was like in 1836. The *Real Reads* version cannot encompass such a broad view, but it does include the most important issues of the day, and the main strands of the plot. Here are the most important subplots that we have had to leave out of the *Real Reads* version.

● The *Real Reads* version leaves out Jim Ratcliffe, a convicted criminal who becomes the turnkey in the Heart of Midlothian, in a cynical but practical move on the part of the magistrates.

- Scott often refers to David Deans' past, when Deans fought against the government for religious freedom. David argues with other characters, always taking a strictly religious point of view. He's even uncertain whether Jeanie should be a witness in court, because the Courts of Justice are a secular (that is, non-religious) institution.

- Scott makes Madge Wildfire an important character, as she quotes many songs and ballads that come from an older, more lawless Scotland.

- A lengthy subplot reveals that Robertson is actually the son of an English clergyman. Effie and Robertson eventually return to Scotland, with Robertson now in the role of an English gentleman.

- The last section only occurs in the *Real Reads* version. Scott actually never writes from the Whistler's point of view, though the details included here are from Scott's original. For example, Meg Murdockson and Madge Wildfire waylay Jeanie on her journey to London and, before she escapes, Jeanie learns that Robertson had been Madge's lover before he was Effie's, and that they had a child which died. Madge's madness dates from Robertson's desertion. It is Jeanie, not the Whistler, who witnesses the hanging of Meg, and the death of Madge, on her way home from London.

● The *Real Reads* version omits the final section of the novel, which describes Jeanie and Reuben's married life and their children.

Back in time

Until 1707 Scotland and England each had their own parliament. In that year the two countries united to form Great Britain with one parliament in London, where all the important decisions were taken.

In 1736, when this story takes place, many Scots still regretted their loss of independence, and felt they were less well off than the English. There was resentment against the London government, which in turn viewed Scotland with suspicion. Only twenty-one years earlier Scottish Jacobites tried to overthrow the British royal family, the Hanoverians, and replace them with the old

Stuart line of kings. The current King, George II, who ruled the German state of Hanover as well as Great Britain, and his Queen, Caroline, shared this suspicion of the Scots.

Although there was an elected parliament, only the wealthy could vote, and it was very difficult for ordinary people to get their voice heard unless they knew someone with influence. That is why Jeanie Deans approaches the powerful Scottish nobleman, the Duke of Argyll, as she attempts to save her sister's life.

The church, or Kirk, was very powerful, and played a central role in national life. It was taken for granted that everyone believed in God – within living memory people had been executed for questioning God's existence. It would have been unthinkable for Scott not to have given God a capital G. Kings and governments frequently tried to control the Kirk, but this often provoked popular resistance. David Deans was a Covenanter, one of a group who had fought to defend what he believed was the proper way of worshipping God.

The legal system was very cruel. People could be put to death for a wide variety of crimes. In *The Heart of Midlothian*, Walter Scott, a lawyer as well as a writer, draws on two real cases from the previous hundred years. One was the trial, reprieve and lynching of Porteous, the Captain of the Town Guard; the other was the case of a young woman who, like Effie Deans, faced execution for the crime of keeping her pregnancy secret. Her sister, Helen Walker, like Jeanie Deans in Scott's story, walked to London to secure a royal pardon.

The legal system was also unjust. Porteous, who had shot innocent people, was spared execution because of powerful friends in high places, while Effie faced death because her sister was too honest to tell the lie which would have saved her.

Edinburgh, which was then the most important city in Scotland, was still relatively small and cramped, and the mob was notoriously violent. Most people lived in tall tenement buildings in narrow closes or alleys running off the main street which ran from the castle, past St Giles High

Kirk and through the Canongate, to Holyrood Palace. Close to St Giles was the prison, the Heart of Midlothian. The site where it stood is still marked by a heart-shaped pattern of cobblestones. The name lived on in many Edinburgh institutions including a nineteenth-century dancing society, whose members went on to found the football club of the same name.

The Heart of Midlothian is famous for its historically accurate account of the Porteous riots. Robertson and Wilson were real people, though there is also a large cast of fictional characters who give a general sense of Edinburgh society.

Finding out more

We recommend the following books and websites to help you gain a better understanding of Walter Scott, his world and his novels:

Books

● David Carroll, *Ten Tales From Dumfries and Galloway*, 2010. One tale is that of Helen Walker, the real person on whom Scott based Jeanie Deans.

- Eileen Dunlop, *Supernatural Scotland*, Scotties Books, 2011.

- Anne Bruce English, *Let's Explore Edinburgh Old Town*, Luath Press, 2001.

- Joshua Parry, *Edinburgh Unlocked*, 2010.

- Hew Smith, *Scottish Songs, Ballads and Poems*, 2007.

- Claire Watts, *The Covenanters*, Scotties Books, 2011.

Websites

- www.scotster.com/forums/scottish-local-history/The-Porteous-Riots-1736.3833.html
A website about the Porteous Riots.

- www.electricscotland.com/history/women/walker_helen.htm
A website about Helen Walker, whose story gave Scott the idea for Jeanie Deans.

- www.bbc.co.uk/scotland/history/covenanters
The BBC website about the Covenanters.

- www.shc.ed.ac.uk/Research/witches/

A website about Scottish witchcraft, and people like Madge Wildfire.

Food for thought

Starting points

- Do you think Jeanie was right to refuse to tell a lie, even if it would save Effie's life?

- If a law made by government is unjust, are people justified in taking the law into their own hands?

- Should a government be allowed to make laws about people's religious beliefs?

- Was it a disadvantage for the Scots to have both their king and parliament in London rather than in Edinburgh?

- Should the law ever have the right to kill people?

Language and style

- Find some examples of Scots words and sentences. Can you tell what they mean? Try reading them aloud. How do they sound?

- Would it have been better for the person retelling this story to translate all the Scots language into English?

- There is a lot of dialogue in *The Heart of Midlothian*. Choose a piece of dialogue which you find interesting or exciting and try acting it out loud as if you were the character speaking. This often works best if there are two of you to take different parts. Does this change the way you enjoy and understand the story?

- Do you find anything in *The Heart of Midlothian* scary? Is there anything about the way it's written that makes it even more frightening?

Narrative

The story is told by a third-person narrator. This means it is not told by any of the characters, but by someone quite outside the events that are described.

Can you ever tell what this third-person narrator thinks about the people and events in the story? The list of themes below might help you to answer this question.

Does the third-person narrator ever tell parts of the story from the point of view of a particular character? Can you find a place where this happens? What difference does it make to the way you see the events?

Themes

What do you think Sir Walter Scott is saying about the following themes in *The Heart of Midlothian*?

- right and wrong
- law and justice
- religion and morality
- violence
- Scotland and England
- singing and dancing